This edition published 2010 by Zero to Ten Ltd,
Part of the Evans Publishing Group,
2A Portman Mansions,
Chiltern Street,
London, W1U 6NR

British Library Cataloguing in Publication Data
A CIP catalogue record for this book is available
from the British Library

ISBN: 9781840895827

Printed in China by New Era Printing Co. Ltd

Terry the Flying Turtle

by Anna Wilson

illustrated by Mike Gordon

ZERO TO TEN

"I'm clever," said Terry the Turtle. Polly the Chimp laughed.

Terry was cross.
"I **am** clever," said Terry.
"I can fly."

Polly laughed and laughed.
"You can't fly!" she said.

Terry was cross.
"I **can** fly," he said.
"You'll see."

"Will you help me?"
Terry asked the parrot.
"I want to fly."

The parrot laughed.
Terry was cross.
"Please will
you help me?"
he asked.

"All right," said the parrot.
"Hold this twig and I'll
hold it too."

"Why?" asked Terry.

"Because it will help you fly," said the parrot.

The parrot held on.
Terry held on.

The parrot flew.
Terry flew!

The animals watched.
"Look at Terry!" they said.
"He looks silly!"

Terry was cross.
"I'm not silly," he shouted.
"You're silly. I'm flying!"

Terry fell down
and down.

SPLASH!

"You look silly now!" Polly said.